Trail Blazers

Life in Space

by Helen Orme

Ransom

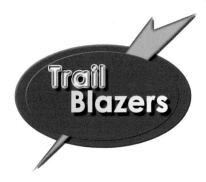

Trailblazers

Life in Space
by Helen Orme
Educational consultant: Helen Bird

Illustrated by Jorge Mongiovi

Published by Ransom Publishing Ltd.
51 Southgate Street, Winchester, Hants. SO23 9EH
www.ransom.co.uk

ISBN   978 184167 690 6
First published in 2009

Life in Space

Contents

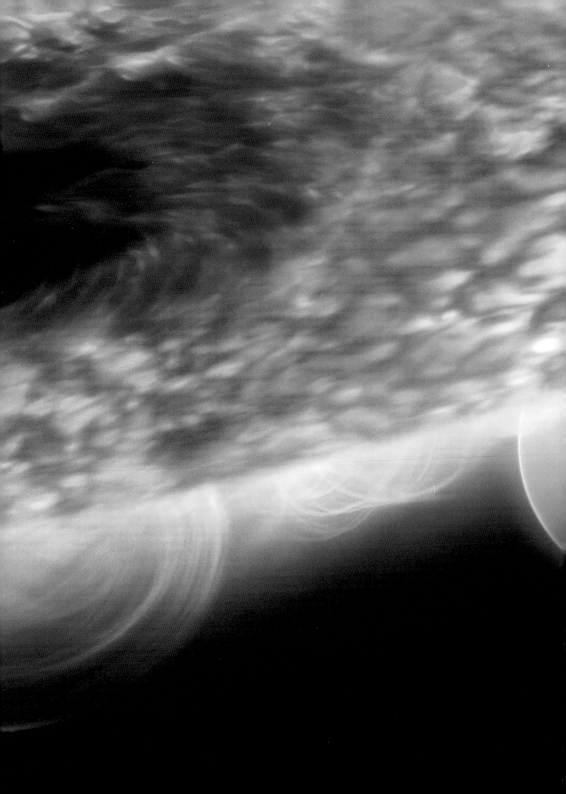

Life in Space

Get the facts

What do you need for life?

Water

Life

Life needs water!

Why?

Living things are made of cells.

Water

Cells need to:

- move things around.

- change chemicals from one sort to another.

The only way this can be done is with water.

The water must be **liquid**, so the temperature must be right – not too hot, not too cold.

There is plenty of water in the universe. But it is only liquid in a few places.

Energy

Life cannot exist without energy. But it needs to be the right amount of energy; not too much, and not too little.

On Earth, our energy comes from the Sun. Plants use this energy to change air and water into the stuff they need to grow.

Earth

Are water and energy all that living things need?

No. The universe is mainly made of an element called hydrogen. Living things need other elements too, such as carbon.

Where do these elements come from?

They are made inside stars.

So our bodies are made of **star dust!**

That's right! Without stars, we wouldn't be here!

Life in the Solar System

Why is Earth right for life?

The Earth is a great place for life.

It is the right distance from the Sun. The temperature on the Earth is just right for water to be liquid most of the time.

Earth has an atmosphere. Over millions of years, living things have changed the atmosphere so it is just right for their needs.

An atmosphere is important to protect living things from dangerous radiation from the Sun.

Where else might there be life?

Mars

Astrobiologists (scientists who study life in space) say that Mars once had liquid water.

There may have been life on the planet once. Some simple life may still be there.

This rock came from Mars.

Some scientists think that it shows the remains of living things.

Europa

Europa is a moon of **Jupiter**.

It is covered with ice. Under the ice there may be water. This water might be kept liquid by **underwater volcanoes**.

Scientists are planning a mission to land on Europa and drill down through the ice to look for life.

Pic.: The surface of Mars.

Finding life around other stars

We know that there are many planets in the universe.

Astronomers are now finding planets the size of the Earth. If they are the right distance from their sun, they may have life. This life may even be **intelligent**!

How will we know if there is life around other stars?

Planets that are the right size for life are **too small** to be studied. But **one day** we will be able to study them. We will find out if these planets are made of the chemicals needed for **life**.

10

Getting in touch

A journey to another star would take **thousands of years**.

So we will never be in touch with aliens?

We could talk to them by **radio**. Radio waves travel at the speed of light. It would take just over **four years** to send a message to the nearest star.

There are two problems

- It would take another four years to get a reply.

- They may not understand what we are trying to say to them!

The Arecibo Receiver

This telescope is listening for messages from space. So far, they haven't found any.

Life on Earth
– how we got here

How did life start?

The Earth was very different **four billion years ago**. We couldn't have lived then. There was **no oxygen** in the atmosphere.

Chemicals in the air and water began to join together. **Heat** and **lightning** may have made this happen.

This took millions of years.

At some point a **simple cell** was formed. This was able to make copies of itself. This was the **beginning of life**.

Life

Q Why aren't new types of life still being made?

A The mix of chemicals is very different now.

A different idea – life from space

Maybe life didn't start on Earth at all, but arrived from space.

Meteorites have been found that have the chemicals that make life inside them.

Some scientists say that life could have started on Mars first, then spread to Earth.

Remember that Martian meteorite on page 9?

A different belief – intelligent design

Some people believe that life on Earth didn't just happen by chance. They say that complicated things, like cars or computers, can't happen by accident. They are designed by somebody.

Living things are even more complicated. They must have been designed too.

So what is true? Read, think, and decide for yourself!

Most scientists don't agree. They say that evolution, over millions of years, can do the job just as well as a designer.

Weird life – extremophiles

Some living things on Earth can be found in very extreme places. Some fish and insects can live in the total darkness of caves.

A blind cave fish

Lungfish can bury themselves in mud when the lake or river they are in dries up.

They can stay buried in the mud for years.

Some **worms** in the Antarctic spend most of their lives 'freeze-dried'. They blow about in the wind for years until conditions are right.

14

Bacteria are tiny, but they are extreme survivors! Here are some places where types of bacteria are found:

- In boiling water.
- Where there is dangerous radiation.
- Where there is no oxygen or no water.
- Extremely hot and cold places.
- On the Moon! (*NASA found bacteria on a space probe from Earth that had survived on the Moon.*)
- On hot, bare rocks in deserts.

Why are extremophiles important?

They show that life is possible in **extreme places**. This means that life may exist on planets that are not like the Earth.

They show that simple life can survive in space, so bacteria could travel from one planet to another.

Why is the universe right for life?

The planet Earth is **just right** for life.

So is the universe.

The universe works in the way it does because of different forces, like **gravity** and the forces that stop atoms falling apart.

If any of these forces worked just a little bit differently, life couldn't happen.

Why not?

If gravity was just a tiny bit stronger, the universe could not have expanded. **Stars** wouldn't have been made. That would mean that the elements needed for life could not have been made.

 If the forces inside atoms were stronger or weaker, the **molecules** that make living things would be impossible.

16.

So how come the universe ended up just right for life?

Some people have come up with the idea that our universe was created inside a **giant computer** by brilliantly clever aliens.

(Let's hope they don't turn the computer off!)

Some people say the designer is **God**.

What do you think?

There is a problem with the idea that someone designed the universe.

Who designed **them** in the first place?

We don't know. But here are some ideas:

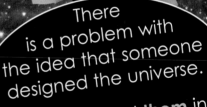 We **just got lucky**.

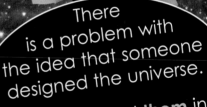 Maybe there are **millions of universes!** Our universe is the one that is just right for life. That's why we're here.

 It was **designed that way**. *(We talked about a designer on page 13.)*

Chapter 1:
Life is rare

'This star has eight planets,' said the science officer. 'Let's visit the third one. It's the right distance from the sun for life.'

The team of space explorers were searching the galaxy for life. It wasn't easy to find. Planets were too near the sun, too far away, too big or too small, or made of the wrong things.

Life was rare in the universe.

The planet had a thick atmosphere, without much oxygen. It didn't look like a place where they would find life, but the captain decided to land anyway. The explorers had found life in some very strange places before.

The navigator used radar to find a safe place to land. The space ship settled down on the top of a high crag.

That was when the problems started.

Chapter 2:
The accident

The ship had four strong landing legs to make it stand level. Three of the legs hit solid rock, but the fourth landed on loose rocks. The ship slipped to one side. Part of the ship hit the ground with a crash.

The crew quickly put on their space suits in case the air leaked out of the ship.

They were all very worried. What if they couldn't take off again? Would they die on this planet, many light-years from home?

The crew went outside and the engineer checked the damage.

'It's not too bad,' he said. 'It's going to take a while to fix, but we can handle it.'

'Looks like we are going to have plenty of time to explore this planet!' said the science officer. 'But I don't think it is going to be very interesting!'

Chapter 3:
A young planet

The space ship had a small, two-person aircraft. The navigator and the chief scientist would explore the planet. The rest of the crew stayed behind to help the engineer fix the space ship.

The aircraft took off. The captain talked to them by radio.

'Take care. With the space ship damaged, we can't come and rescue you if you get into trouble.'

The view from the aircraft was amazing.

They were near the shore of an ocean. Huge volcanoes sent up great clouds of smoke and dust. Burning lava poured down into the water, sending up clouds of steam. Overhead, dark clouds streamed by, pushed by powerful winds.

'The surface of this planet is just forming,' said the science officer. 'It's much too early to find life here.'

They turned back to the space ship.

Chapter 4:
Life begins

The repair work was finished. The ship's cook was clearing up after a meal. The captain was getting ready to take off.

The cook looked at all the left-over scraps.

'No point in taking this into space,' he thought. 'I'll leave it behind on the planet.'

He put on his space suit and carried the waste bin out of the airlock. He tipped the scraps out on to the rocks.

There *had* been no life on the planet. But there was now.

Three and a half billion years later, the planet was a very different place.

The seas were full of life. Forests had spread over the land. Huge cities had sprung up.

A huge rocket stood ready to blast off into space.

A team of space explorers were ready to search the galaxy for life.

Life in Space word check

alien

atmosphere

bacteria

centigrade

chemical

designer

element

energy

explorer

extremophile

hydrogen

intelligent

light-year

liquid

oxygen

radiation

survivor

temperature

universe

volcano